The Case of the
Stolen Baseball Cards

Read all the Jigsaw Jones Mysteries

Coming Soon

The Case of the
Stolen Baseball Cards

by James Preller
illustrated by John Speirs
cover illustration by R. W. Alley

A
LITTLE APPLE
PAPERBACK

SCHOLASTIC INC.
New York Toronto London Auckland Sydney
Mexico City New Delhi Hong Kong

Dedicated to the memory
of Raymond Chandler,
for the creation of the
greatest gumshoe
of them all,
Philip Marlowe

Book design by Dawn Adelman

No part of this publication may be reproduced in whole or in part, or stored in a retrieval system, or transmitted in any form or by any means, electronic, mechanical, photocopying, recording, or otherwise, without written permission of the publisher. For information regarding permission, write to Scholastic Inc., Attention: Permissions Department, 555 Broadway, New York, NY 10012.

ISBN 0-439-08083-5

12 11 10 9 8 7 6 5 4 3 2   9/9 0 1 2 3 4/0

Printed in the U.S.A.   40
First Scholastic printing, July 1999

Contents

Chapter One
Eddie's Baseball Cards

I got up. I got out of bed. I dragged a comb across my head.

Wednesday morning — oh, brother. It was as exciting as a bowl of oatmeal.

Here's the thing. I was a detective without a case. That's like being a hamburger without a bun. It's like being Mike Piazza without a pitch to hit. I needed a mystery to solve. I mean, what good is a detective if he isn't fighting crime?

I sat at the breakfast table, drinking grape juice and waiting for the toaster to

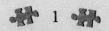 1

pop. The sky was as blue as a swimming pool. A voice on the radio was talking about Indian summer. I checked the backyard. No Apaches in sight.

"It's not fair," my eleven-year-old brother, Nicholas, moaned. "Kids shouldn't have to go to school on nice days like today."

"Yeah," my oldest brother, Billy, agreed. "We should all take the day off and drive up to the lake. What do you say, Dad?"

My father looked up from his newspaper and frowned. "I wish we could," he said. "But we can't. So stop complaining and eat your breakfast."

That was my dad for you. He was an ogre in the morning. In the Jones family, we've learned to give Dad plenty of room until he drinks his coffee. But after that — *abracadabra* — he turns into a pretty great dad. That coffee sure works wonders.

After polishing off my second plate of frozen miniwaffles, I hurried to the bus

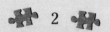

stop. Mila skipped out of her house when I arrived. She was lucky — the bus stopped in front of her house.

As usual, Mila was singing:

> *"Oh, take me out to the ball game,*
> *Take me out to the crowd.*
> *Buy me some peanuts and pizza,*
> *I don't care if we never get back."*

"Pizza?" I asked. "Don't you mean Cracker Jacks?"

"I like pizza better," Mila explained. "Cracker Jacks get trapped in my teeth."

Mila and I are in Ms. Gleason's class together — room 201. But we aren't just classmates. We are partners. We solve mysteries together.

For a dollar a day, we make problems go away.

When the bus pulled up, I suddenly realized I had my own problem to solve. I forgot my lunch box. That meant buying hot lunch in the school cafeteria. Oh, brother, mystery meatballs again.

Yeesh.

There was a crowd of kids already on the bus. Mila and I walked to the back and sat down. Eddie Becker had a blue binder open on his lap. Everybody was leaning over their seats to see it.

Eddie bragged, "Smart baseball card

collectors, like me and my uncle Max, collect rookie cards."

"Wow, you've got Sammy Sosa!" Mike Radcliffe exclaimed. "Slammin' Sammy is my favorite!"

Kim Lewis, her wild hair flying out from underneath a Yankees cap, squealed when she saw Derek Jeter's rookie card. "He's *sooooo* awesome!"

Mila said to me, "That Eddie's got a great collection. I bet it's worth a lot of money."

"Big whoop-de-do," I mumbled.

I'll be honest. I wasn't exactly president of the Eddie Becker Fan Club. I thought he was a show-off. And you didn't need to be a detective to see it. The proof was right there at the back of the bus.

Chapter Two

Stolen!

All the kids in room 201 acted like Eddie's baseball card collection was the greatest thing since Nintendo.

Trust me. It wasn't.

I was so not interested. I had to tackle the Lunch Problem. I walked up to Ms. Gleason's desk and tried to look as sad as possible. "I forgot my lunch," I moaned. "I might not make it."

Ms. Gleason chuckled to herself. "You remind me of my basset hound. He makes the same face when he wants something.

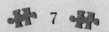

Don't worry. Before lunch you can take a buddy to the secretary's office. Mrs. Vega will give you a dollar from petty cash."

That was a relief. Sure, I might be poisoned from eating mystery meatballs. But at least I wouldn't starve to death.

Suddenly I heard Eddie's voice get loud and angry. "Hey, don't grab!" he told Bobby Solofsky. "That card's in mint condition."

"Mint condition?" Bobby said. "It's got jelly stains on it!"

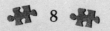

Ms. Gleason interrupted, "Look with your eyes, boys and girls. Remember our classroom rules." She pointed to a poster on the wall. She read rule number nine, *"Respect other people's things."*

The bell rang. We stood for the Pledge of Allegiance. When we were all seated, Eddie walked over to the closet. He looked at Ms. Gleason, shrugged, and explained, "I forgot something." Eddie hung his backpack on a hook and slid his blue binder onto the top shelf.

Eddie Becker had blond hair and blue eyes — and he was crazy about baseball. Eddie wore the same baseball shirt every single day. He knew every statistic for all the players. Eddie Becker was a walking, talking baseball encyclopedia. But I think he loved his baseball cards most of all.

When Eddie returned to his seat, Ms. Gleason announced, "Today we're going to start a new project called 'All About Me.'"

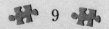

She reached down behind her desk and lifted up a suitcase.

"All right, field trip!" Ralphie Jordan piped up. "We're going to Disney World!"

Everybody laughed, even Ms. Gleason. "I thought it would be nice if we could get to know one another a little better," Ms. Gleason said. "First I'll share some things about me." One by one, Ms. Gleason took things out of her suitcase. She showed us her running sneakers, ski goggles, a jar of seashells, and a few photographs. There was even one of her in a basketball uniform!

"Wow," Athena Lorenzo said. "Did you play in the WNBA, Ms. Gleason?"

Ms. Gleason laughed. "No, the WNBA wasn't around when I played," she said. "But I did play college ball."

Ms. Gleason told us about Brutus, her basset hound. Those are the goofy-looking dogs with short legs and long ears. "He's a

piece of work," Ms. Gleason said. "Brutus will eat anything — even my smelly socks!" Everybody laughed. I liked that Ms. Gleason had a dog. My dad says there are two kinds of people in the world: dog people and cat people. He says that I'm a dog person. I was glad to learn that Ms. Gleason was a dog person, too.

Ms. Gleason pulled out a banner made out of construction paper and tacked it to the wall. The banner had her name on it and lots of crayon pictures. The pictures, she told us, were of her favorite hobbies.

"Tonight for homework," Ms. Gleason said, "I'd like you to make your own banners." She even gave us our own blank banners to fill in at home.

When the rest of the class lined up for lunch, I went with Ralphie Jordan to the secretary's office. Then we went to meet our class in the cafeteria.

After lunch we played outside for a

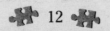

while. Ms. Gleason usually reads to us after recess, so we plopped down on the carpet in the reading circle. Playing was hard work and we were all a little tired.

While we waited for story time, Eddie got up to check on his collection. He pulled down the binder, opened it, and exclaimed: "My cards! They're gone!"

He held up the binder for everyone to see.

The pages were empty!

Chapter Three

The Phantom Leaves a Clue

Eddie looked around the room. "Somebody stole my baseball cards!"

No one said a word. We just sat there, shocked.

"Who did it?" Eddie demanded. "Was it you, Bigs?" Eddie pointed an accusing finger at Bigs Maloney. "Or was it you, Kim? You're the one who made such a fuss over my Derek Jeter card."

Ms. Gleason spoke up. "That's enough, Eddie," she said in a stern voice. "No one is pointing fingers in my classroom."

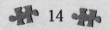

"But —"

"No buts," Ms. Gleason said, her face turning red. "I know you're upset. But please return to your seat. I'll handle this."

Mila raised her hand. "Excuse me, Ms. Gleason!" she said.

"What is it, Mila?"

Mila stood up. "When Eddie picked up the binder, I noticed that a scrap of paper fell to the ground. Maybe it's a clue."

Eddie rushed over to pick up the paper. He read it, then held up the note for everyone to see. It read:

Everybody started talking at once, until Ms. Gleason made us settle down. Ms. Gleason was unhappy, and she didn't try to hide it. The kids were worried and upset.

After all, there was a thief in room 201.

I took out my detective journal. I couldn't find my red marker. So I picked up my next favorite color. I wrote in green:

The Case of the Stolen Baseball Cards.

Below that, I made two neat columns. At the top of one, I wrote Suspects. On the other, I wrote Clues.

I turned to a new page and wrote:

Who is the Phantom????

Meanwhile, Ms. Gleason went over to Eddie and talked to him quietly. Then she stood up in front of the class. "Boys and girls, this is serious. Eddie says he had twenty-six baseball cards in his binder."

"He did," Helen Zuckerman chimed in. "We all saw them."

Ms. Gleason nodded. "Okay," she said. "The cards are missing, and I'm very, very upset. We all know never to touch someone's personal property. But maybe someone took the cards by accident. Please look in your desks."

No one found a thing. Except Joey Pignattano. He found an old Oreo stuffed in the back of his desk. Joey twisted it open,

licked the white insides, and gobbled down the cookie part in two bites.

I scribbled a message to Mila in secret code. It was pretty easy to read, once you knew the trick. You had to cross out every other letter. That's why detectives call it an Alternate Letter Code.

I handed the page to Mila. It looked like this:

MQEWERTY MUEP ASTA TFHJEL
OMFBFCIZCTEI ALFKTHEDRR SXCVHZOKOPL.

Here's what it really said:

M~~Q~~E~~W~~E~~R~~T~~Y~~ M~~U~~E~~P~~ A~~S~~T~~A~~ T~~F~~H~~J~~E~~L~~
O~~M~~F~~B~~F~~C~~I~~Z~~C~~T~~E~~I~~ A~~L~~F~~K~~T~~H~~E~~D~~R~~R~~ S~~X~~C~~V~~H~~Z~~O~~K~~O~~P~~L.

Chapter Four

A Bargain

After reading the note, Mila slid a finger across her nose. That was our secret signal. In the detective business, you can't be too careful. That's why we use codes and secret signals. I looked around the room. Bigs Maloney, Joey Pignattano, Lucy Hiller, even my pal Ralphie Jordan — anyone might be the Phantom.

Out on the playground for afternoon recess, everybody was talking about the robbery. Most kids felt bad for Eddie. But Kim Lewis was mad. She said Eddie was wrong to accuse her. I agreed with Kim. You

can't accuse someone until you have proof. Solving a mystery is like doing a jigsaw puzzle. It's not solved until all the pieces are in place.

I wanted to talk to Eddie Becker — *alone*. But I had to wait for him to finish talking with Bigs Maloney. I couldn't hear what they were saying, but Bigs looked pretty unhappy. I guessed that Bigs didn't like being accused, either. Believe me, you don't want to mess with Bigs Maloney. We didn't call him "Bigs" for nothing.

I finally grabbed Eddie and handed him my business card. Actually, it was an index card with Mila's neat handwriting on it:

| Need a Mystery Solved? |
| Call Jigsaw Jones |
| or Mila Yeh, |
| Private Eyes! |
| For a Dollar a Day, |
| We Make Problems Go Away!!! |

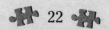

Eddie looked at the card and yawned. He handed it back to me. "No thanks," he said.

"Don't you want your baseball cards found?" I asked.

Eddie stared at me for a minute. Then he smiled. "Tell you what," he said. "If you want to try to solve this case, that's fine with me. But I won't pay you."

"Sorry, Eddie," I said. "It doesn't work that way."

Eddie scratched at the ground with his sneaker. "I'll make a deal with you" he said. "If you solve the mystery, you can have any one of my baseball cards. But if you don't solve it by tomorrow," he said, "you have to pay me a dollar."

"Tomorrow," I said. "That's rough."

"Well, if you can't do it . . ."

"*Any* card?" I asked.

"You can take your pick," Eddie answered.

"It's a deal." We sealed it with a handshake.

"Let me see the Phantom's note," I said. Eddie handed over the paper. I studied it under my magnifying glass. I slipped the note into my pocket. "I'll keep this," I said. "It's evidence."

Eddie shrugged. He didn't seem to care one way or the other.

Finally it was the end of the school day. Everybody had jobs to do in room 201. We all had to clean up our area and sharpen our pencils. Plus, some kids got special jobs. There were Homework Checkers and Closet Neateners, Board Cleaners and Eraser Stampers and chair Putter-Uppers.

Mila was the Homework Checker that day. Me and Ralphie were Chair Putter-Uppers. Danika Starling was Zookeeper. We had two hamsters in our class, Romeo and Juliet, and they needed food and fresh water every day. We all agreed: Zookeeper was the best job in the classroom.

When we lined up to leave, Ms. Gleason said, "Before you go, boys and girls, I want everybody to empty their backpacks. It's a good time to clean out old papers."

Ms. Gleason didn't fool me for a minute. I knew that she was still hoping to find Eddie's missing baseball cards. We all dumped out our packs. But there were no cards to be found.

"I'm sorry, Eddie," Ms. Gleason said. "They don't seem to be anywhere."

I wasn't surprised.

The Phantom wasn't going to be caught that easily.

Chapter Five

In the Tree House

Mila met me at my tree house after school. I could hear her coming from a mile away. She sang:

"Root, root, root for the home team,
If they don't win, it's a bummer.
'Cause it's one, two, three strikes you're out
At the old ball game!"

Mila climbed up the tree house ladder. I handed her my magnifying glass and the note. "The paper's torn," I said. "And look."

I pointed to the red and blue lines on the page. "It's the same kind of paper we use for homework."

Mila studied the note. "Red marker," she murmured. Mila rocked back and forth, thinking. "The writing is all squiggly and wiggly," she said.

"Yeah, like it was written by a first-grader," I said.

Mila ran her fingers through her long black hair. "Or maybe," she said, "the

Phantom did it on purpose."

"Could be," I said. "Handwriting is like a fingerprint. The Phantom probably wrote it extra sloppy as a disguise. Too bad," I sighed. "I guess this isn't much of a clue."

That's when Mila turned the paper over. "Hey, Jigsaw," she said. "Look at this."

There were some letters, written neatly in pencil, on the back.

"Yeah," I said. "So?"

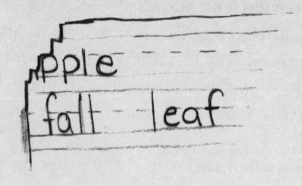

"Jigsaw, don't you remember?" Mila said. "These are some of the words from last night's vocabulary homework."

"pple?" I asked. "What's a *pple*?"

"The page is torn," Mila said. "The front letter is missing."

I thought for a minute. Then I thought for another. I was on my third minute of Deep Thinking when Mila blurted out, *"Apple!"*

"I was just about to say that," I complained.

"There's something else," Mila said. "I recognize this handwriting. This page came from Kim's homework!"

Chapter Six
Kim's Story

I opened my detective journal. "Now we're getting somewhere. Boy, I'm good at this detective stuff." I poked Mila in the ribs. "Just kidding, Mila. Nice work."

Mila looked down, embarrassed.

Under the word Suspects, I wrote the name Kim Lewis. I circled it in orange. "Kim's our best suspect," I said. "Eddie also accused Bigs Maloney." I wrote down his name, too.

"It could be anybody," Mila said. "Even you."

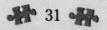

"Me?" I said.

Mila smiled. "Well, it is written in marker — and everyone knows you always carry around a set of markers. Plus," she added, "when the whole class went to the cafeteria, you were walking the hallways. You could have stolen it then."

"You don't really think . . ."

"Nah." Mila laughed. "I can be a kidder, too, you know."

For a joke, I added my name to the list of suspects. Then I said in a deep voice, "Jigsaw Jones, did you do it?" I answered myself, "Nope. I'm innocent."

I crossed out my name. "He says he didn't do it," I told Mila.

She just shook her head.

I slugged down the last of my grape juice. "We need more facts," I concluded. "Let's go have a little talk with Kim Lewis."

Kim lived three blocks away. On the way

over, Mila and I discussed the case. I told her about my deal with Eddie.

"Hmmm," Mila said.

"What do you mean *hmmm*?" I asked.

"Nothing," Mila answered, "Just *hmmm*."

I stopped. "Well? Is it a good *hmmm* . . . or a bad *hmmm*?!"

Mila lifted her shoulders and let them drop. "It's just a *hmmm-hmmm*."

Oh, brother. We walked on. "I saw Bigs Maloney and Eddie talking on the

playground," I said. "Bigs didn't look too happy."

"Bigs scares me," Mila said. "He's so . . ."

". . . big," I said, finishing her sentence. I didn't tell Mila that Bigs scared me, too. Because he didn't. I knew the big lug was basically a nice guy. He just . . . sort of . . . made me a little . . . *nervous*.

Kim was playing catch with Nicole Rodriguez. They were practicing their grounders and pop-ups. They were pretty good.

"Hey, guys, want to play?" Kim shouted.

"Can't," I said. "We're on a case."

Kim threw a high pop to Nicole.

I showed Kim the note — but only the side with her handwriting on it. "Recognize this?" I asked.

Across the yard, Nicole made a nice running catch.

"Time-out!" Kim yelled. She looked closely at the note. "Hey, that's from my

homework. Where'd you get this?"

I turned the note over. Kim read the words: THE PHANTOM STRIKES!

Kim looked at us, confused. "I don't understand," she said.

I got right to the point. "Are you the Phantom?"

"No," Kim said, smiling. "I'm the Easter Bunny!" She jutted out her front teeth and hopped across the yard.

Yeesh. I was surrounded by loonies.

Mila interrupted, "Kim, I was the Homework Checker today. You didn't hand in your homework."

Kim stopped hopping. "Do you think I stole Eddie's cards?" she said. "Nice friends. Thanks a lot — and see ya later."

Kim started walking away. "Come on, Nicole. We're out of here."

Mila called after her, "Don't get mad, Kim. We didn't mean . . ."

Kim spun around. "Listen, I did my

homework last night. I brought it to school. Then I lost it. End of story."

"Lost it?" Mila asked. "When?"

Kim made a face. "If I knew that, I wouldn't have lost it." She went inside the house with Nicole. The door slammed shut.

"Do you believe her?" Mila asked.

"I don't know," I answered. "Maybe, maybe not."

Mila closed her eyes, lifted her chin, and let the sun's warm rays wash over her face. She frowned. "I've got to get home," she said. "We've done enough damage for today."

"Go ahead," I said. "I'm going to catch up with Bigs Maloney."

"Good luck, Jigsaw," Mila said.

"Yeah," I answered. "I'll need it."

Chapter Seven

A Pain in the Neck

Mrs. Maloney answered the door. She held one baby in her arms. Another baby was on the ground, grabbing her leg. "You've met the twins, haven't you?" she asked. "This is Harry. And the little guy sucking on my knee is Larry."

That's the thing with twins. They all look alike. To make things worse, Harry and Larry dressed alike. "How do you tell who's who?" I asked.

"Oh, a mother knows," Mrs. Maloney

said. "But here's a tip: Larry has a big freckle on his nose. Harry doesn't."

"Is Bigs home?" I asked.

"Yes, he's in the family room. He's supposed to be doing his homework." She wiped Harry's nose with a tissue. "But I think he's watching television."

I found Bigs in the family room. There was no homework in sight. But that wasn't the weird thing. Bigs was dressed in red long johns and a red long-sleeved shirt. He

wore blue underwear on top of his long johns. Bigs wore a mask over his face. And a black cape.

The letter *P* was taped to his chest.

Bigs was jumping up and down on the couch, throwing fake punches. He was watching a wrestling match on TV.

"Jigsaw, you gotta see this," Bigs urged. "The Red Phantom is about to pin the Terrorizer!"

I didn't have much choice. You don't

argue with Bigs Maloney. After the match, Bigs clicked off the TV. "Let's wrestle," he said. "I'll be the Red Phantom. You can be the Terrorizer."

"Er, but Bigs," I stammered. "Wrestling isn't really my —"

Wham! Before I knew it, Bigs pounced on me. Then he twisted my body into the shape of a pretzel.

"Pinned!" Bigs shouted, thrusting his fists into the air. "The Red Phantom triumphs again!"

He looked down at me. "You all right, Jigsaw?" he asked.

I tried to wiggle my fingers. They still worked. "Is there a doctor in the house?" I said.

Bigs laughed. "You're funny."

"Yeah, funny," I groaned.

Bigs helped me up. "I'm going to be a professional wrestler when I grow up," he told me. "Either that . . . or a florist."

"A florist?"

Bigs laid his huge paw on my shoulder. He had the grip of a grizzly bear. "Yeah, what's the matter? You don't like flowers?"

I told Bigs I liked flowers. I *loved* flowers. Some of my best friends were flowers. Finally he released his grip. My shoulder ached. But at least it was still attached to the rest of my body.

"Want to wrestle again?" Bigs asked. "I need to practice my double knee drop."

"Uh, er, I'd love to, really," I said, backing

up. "But I'm in a hurry. I came to ask you a few questions about Eddie Becker."

"Don't even say that guy's name," Bigs said. "He owes me a baseball card. Now Eddie says he can't pay me back."

As Bigs told it, I wasn't the only guy he mangled in a wrestling match. Last week, Bigs and Eddie watched wrestling on TV together. Then Bigs pinned him — six times in a row.

"We made a bet," Bigs said. "If I won, I was allowed to take my pick of his best baseball cards."

I thought it over. "But without any cards," I said, "he can't pay you."

"Almost," Bigs said. "Eddie's still got plenty of cards. But they're all *commons*. I wanted one of his prized rookie cards."

"What's a *common*?" I asked.

"Every year they print thousands of baseball cards," Bigs explained. "Some of them will be worth a lot of money

someday. But most cards," he said, shaking his head, "will never be worth anything. They're called *commons*. Most collectors don't want 'em."

I scribbled notes in my journal. Then I got out of there in a hurry. I didn't know what a double knee drop was — and I sure didn't want to find out.

It sounded painful.

Chapter Eight

Grams

I limped home, aching and tired. This detective business was hard work. My big, clumsy, ever-loving dog jumped up and licked my face. "Rags, no! Stop it! YUCK!"

One minute I was a pretzel. The next, I was a human Popsicle. Oh, brother. I could start my own restaurant.

My mom called to me from the kitchen. "Dinner should be ready soon, Theodore," she said. "Why don't you get cracking on that school project of yours?"

That's my mom for you. Somehow she

always knew about my homework — even when I forgot all about it. I went into my room and pulled out the banner that Ms. Gleason gave us. I wrote my name across the top: **JIGSAW JONES**. I used different colors for each letter. I thought about my favorite hobbies.

I drew a picture of a big magnifying glass. Inside I wrote **Finding Clues**. I drew pieces of a jigsaw puzzle. I wrote **Puzzles**. Then I drew a self-portrait. I wrote **Drawing**.

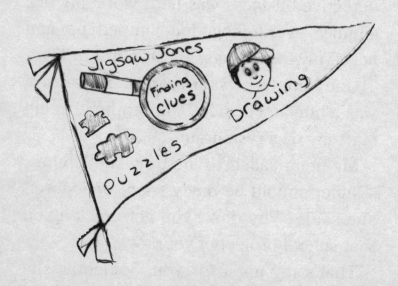

There was a knock on my door. "Dinnertime, Shorty!" That was my sister, Hillary. She's thirteen.

I didn't exactly love being called "Shorty."

But I guess it beats "Peanut."

Grams had everyone laughing at dinner. Grams is my mom's mom. She lives with us now, because after Grandpa died she didn't like being alone. That was fine with me. I love Grams. And besides, she always gives me butterscotch.

Grams told us about the first time my dad picked up Mom for a date. "I didn't like him!" she said, laughing at the memory. "He had a big, bushy beard. He wore dirty jeans with patches all over them. And he had a long ponytail!"

Hillary laughed so hard, she squirted milk through her nose. That made us laugh even more.

"Hey, hey," my dad said. "It was the seventies. Everybody dressed like that."

"I know, dear," Grams said, patting his hand. "You can't judge a man by his clothes. But I'm glad you don't dress like a hippie anymore."

After dinner I asked my mom if she knew anything about baseball cards. "Don't ask me," she said. "Grams is the baseball expert in this house."

"Grams?" I said.

My mom just smiled. "Go ask her," she said.

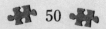

Well, people will surprise you. Just because you see the outside of someone, it doesn't tell you what's *inside*. I guess Grams learned that about my dad. And I was learning it about her.

Grams brought me into her room. She pulled out an old tin from her night table. Inside, wrapped in a rubber band, were some old baseball cards. I mean, *really old* baseball cards.

"Are these worth a lot of money?" I asked her.

Grams waved her hand. "Who knows?" she said. "Probably not. These cards are like me, old and worn-out. Collectors like to keep them in plastic, shiny and new. But I'd never sell them. These cards help me remember the old days."

She touched the tip of my nose with her finger. "When you get to be my age, memories are worth more than money."

We sat and talked for a long time.

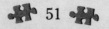 51

Actually, Grams talked. I just listened to her scratchy voice. She told me stories about the old days. About going to Fenway Park with my grandfather to see Ted Williams and the Boston Red Sox. "He was some ballplayer," Grams recalled. "I always loved the Red Sox . . . and I still do."

She got quiet for a while, just picturing it in her mind. The green grass, the noisy crowd, and my grandfather in his wide straw hat. Then she whispered, almost to herself, "Those were happy, happy times."

That's the last thing I remember.

I fell asleep in her lap.

Chapter Nine
Figuring It Out

I woke up in a panic. I dreamed I was being chased by a slobbering, hairy giant. I felt its hot breath on my neck. I felt its claws dig into my back. . . .

I was squished against the wall. My blanket was gone. I rolled over to find Rags hogging the bed. His paws pushed into my back. To make things worse, he was drooling on my pillow.

"Oh, Rags." I sighed. "Give me a break." I tried to push him off. The big fur ball wouldn't budge. Yeesh.

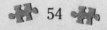

I wondered if cat people had days like this.

I suddenly realized: Today was the day. If I didn't solve the case, I'd owe Eddie Becker a dollar. Time was running out.

I washed and ate breakfast in a hurry.

Briiing, briiing. The phone rang.

"Who could be calling this early?" my mom wondered. She answered the phone, then handed it to me.

"Jigsaw, this is Mila. Can you come right over after breakfast?"

 55

Two minutes later, I was leaning on her doorbell.

Mila and I sat down on her front steps. "A few things about this case have been bothering me," Mila said.

I flicked a pebble with my thumb and listened.

"Eddie didn't seem sad enough," Mila said. "If I lost something that I loved, I'd want to cry."

"Maybe Eddie's not the crying type," I said.

"Maybe," Mila said. "But the thing that really bothers me is how Eddie discovered the robbery."

"What do you mean?" I asked. "He wanted to check on his cards. That's normal."

"I guess," Mila said doubtfully. "But why did he look *inside* the binder? If it was me, I would have checked to see if the binder

was still there. I wouldn't have thought to open it."

Mila had a point. Why did Eddie look inside? Unless . . . Eddie already knew the cards were gone.

I told Mila that Eddie owed Bigs Maloney a baseball card.

Mila smiled. "You found the missing piece, Jigsaw! Eddie had a *motive*."

"A motive?" I asked.

"Yes, a *reason* for faking the robbery! With his best cards stolen," Mila explained, "Eddie wouldn't lose one to Bigs."

It was starting to make sense. "But what about the search?" I asked. "We all had to empty our backpacks."

"*All* of us?" Mila asked. "I don't remember Ms. Gleason looking in *Eddie's* backpack. After all, no one suspected that Eddie stole his own baseball cards."

The bus pulled up.

"I guess Eddie's the Phantom," I concluded. "But we've still got one problem."

"What's that?" Mila asked.

"How did Eddie do it?"

Chapter Ten

The Confession

I sat by the window, watching the world roll past. Eddie was in his usual spot, joking with Bobby Solofsky and Mike Radcliffe. He wore the same identical baseball shirt. Only today I noticed something different. It had an old ink stain on the shoulder.

I thought about Bigs Maloney's twin brothers, Harry and Larry. I thought about Grams — and how the outside of something didn't always tell you what was inside.

And I suddenly knew how Eddie Becker pulled off the crime.

The bus dropped us off at school. We still had a few minutes before class. "Hey, Jigsaw," Eddie called out. "You owe me a dollar." He held out his palm. "Pay up."

A few kids gathered around — Mila, Bobby, Bigs, and Kim Lewis.

I didn't reach into my pocket. "You seem

pretty happy for a guy who lost his best baseball cards," I said.

Eddie let that one pass. "Pay up," he repeated.

I turned to Bigs. "Hey, Bigs," I said. "You ever notice how Eddie always wears the same shirt? Tell me — what kind of guy would wear the same old smelly shirt day after day?"

Eddie shifted on his feet.

"Doesn't your mother ever wash that thing?" I asked him.

"You don't know anything," Eddie said. "I have two of the exact same shirts. When one is in the wash, I wear the clean one."

It was just as I thought. "Except one shirt has an ink stain on the shoulder, right?"

Eddie looked at the stain. "So?"

"So," I said. "You've got two shirts that look alike. No big deal. Bigs has two brothers who look alike. It happens. Except I figure you've got two blue binders that look alike. Don't you, Eddie?"

Eddie's face turned pale.

"Yesterday you brought two blue binders to school, didn't you?" I asked. I held up two fingers. "Not one binder, Eddie. Two."

Eddie turned to leave. "You're crazy."

A large hand with the grip of a grizzly fell on Eddie's shoulder. "Not so fast," Bigs Maloney said.

"Yeah, Eddie," Kim Lewis said. "Not so fast."

Eddie looked at our faces, scared and silent. He was caught, and he knew it.

"One binder had cards," I said. "You made sure to show them to everybody. Then you made the switch. I figure you had an empty blue binder in your backpack. It was a nice trick, Eddie. Especially when you put away the empty binder in the closet for everyone to see. Real smooth.

And the phony note," I said, "that was a nice touch. You had me fooled for a while."

"Is that true, Eddie?" Bigs asked.

Eddie nodded and hung his head. "I'm sorry," he said. "I'm really sorry. It's just . . . well . . . I love those cards so much."

Chapter Eleven

The Phantom Strikes . . . Again!

Mila gave me a high five. "Jigsaw, that was awesome!"

"Thanks," I mumbled.

Even Kim Lewis patted me on the back. "Nice work, detective!" Kim wasn't mad at us anymore.

Ms. Gleason and Eddie talked quietly in the hallway for a long time. None of us could hear a word. And believe me, we tried. When they came back, Eddie looked almost happy — and Ms. Gleason was back to her smiling self.

"Okay, boys and girls," Ms. Gleason said, clapping her hands. "I can't wait to see those banners!"

By the end of the day, room 201 looked like my backyard on laundry day. Our banners dangled from two long ropes stretched across the classroom. They were hung with clothespins. We loved it. Now room 201, Ms. Gleason said, was "All About Us."

After school, I bicycled with Bigs Maloney to Eddie Becker's house. It was payback time. Walking into Eddie's room was like entering the Baseball Hall of Fame. There was a big poster of Mark McGwire, plus hundreds of baseball pictures cut out from magazines. Eddie had baseball bedsheets, baseball trophies, baseball books — even a baseball garbage can.

Eddie had hundreds of cards filed neatly in storage boxes. Those were his commons, the ones that weren't worth much. He kept his best cards in plastic "card guards," stored in three-ring binders.

I didn't waste time. I told Eddie exactly what I wanted. He was thrilled. Eddie happily gave me four quarters and my pick from his commons.

I chose one. "It's not worth anything," Eddie pointed out. "He's just a backup catcher, and the card's not in great shape."

I looked at the card. On the bottom it

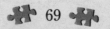

read "Boston Red Sox." I slid it into my pocket. "Maybe not to a collector," I said. "But it will be worth something to a friend of mine."

Bigs, meanwhile, picked out Eddie's most prized treasure. A Ken Griffey Jr. rookie card. Poor Eddie looked like someone had just drowned his cat.

Bigs studied the card, reading all the facts and stats. He looked at poor, miserable Eddie Becker. "I can't take this from you," Bigs said.

"Wh . . . wha . . . what?" Eddie said.

"I can't take it," Bigs said. "You love it too much." He handed the card back to Eddie, who stood there amazed.

"But you still owe me one thing," Bigs said. He jabbed a thick finger at Eddie's chest.

"Sure," Eddie said. "Anything."

Bigs winked at me. "Good," he told Eddie. "Let's wrestle!"

Then Bigs pounced — wham!

I left the room to the sound of Eddie's moans and groans. I heard Bigs Maloney scream, "Pinned! The Red Phantom triumphs again! Get up, Eddie." Bigs urged, "Let's wrestle again!"

I was happy to wrap up another case. I hopped on my bike. First I had to drop off fifty cents at Mila's house. She deserved it. Without her help, I would have never

solved the case. Then I had to find Grams. I had a present for her. It was just a common baseball card, but I knew it would make her smile.

And that was worth more to me than money.

A JIGSAW JONES MYSTERY

by James Preller

Jigsaw and his partner, Mila, know that mysteries are like puzzles—you've got to look at all the pieces to solve the case!

$3.99 Each!

❏ BDE 0-590-69125-2 #1: The Case of Hermie the Missing Hamster

❏ BDE 0-590-69126-0 #2: The Case of the Christmas Snowman

❏ BDE 0-590-69127-9 #3: The Case of the Secret Valentine

❏ BDE 0-590-69129-5 #4: The Case of the Spooky Sleepover

At bookstores everywhere!

Scholastic Inc., P.O. Box 7502, Jefferson City, MO 65102

Please send me the books I have checked above. I am enclosing $_____ (please add $2.00 to cover shipping and handling). Send check or money order—no cash or C.O.D.s please.

Name_____Birthdate_____

Address_____

City_____State/Zip_____

Please allow four to six weeks for delivery. Offer good in U.S.A. only. Sorry, mail orders are not available to residents of Canada. Prices subject to change.